The I

The

Rachel Brown

I dedicate this book in loving memory

of my Grandfather, Charles W. Kraft.

Carol and Ed,

Hallo Reading
Rachel Brown

Table of Contents

Ten rings there are, and nine gold torcs
on the battlechiefs of old
Eight princely virtues, and seven sins
for which a soul is sold
Six is the sum of earth and sky,
of all things meek and bold;
Five is the number of ships
that sailed from Atlantis lost and cold;
Four kings of the Westerlands were saved,
three kingdoms now behold;
Two came together in love and fear
in Llyonesse stronghold
One world there is,
one God, and one birth
the Druid stars foretold

From *Pendragon*, Stephan Lawhead
Oxford, England, 1987

Preface

It's been more than a quarter of a million years since the fall of the Continent Atlantis and another million years for the truth to come to light as the tale of Reigna and her betrothed's love and honesty. The loss of the Atlanteans and the bloodline had been lost to history.

Reigna had been a gifted white witch and a healer who had taken great care of her people even when things looked to be in dire straits and she had known that not everyone can be saved by her kind, sweet, and caring touch. She had resolved to stay as a single woman until her father had given her something she'd never have expected, a betrothed, who was the youngest son of Felicia Korri Eros and Daemion Virgil Eros who had grown up with both Reigna's mother (Regina Krystal Valera) and her father (Regulous Pisces Valera).

Regulous took great care in arranging the meeting and in doing so he made this a beautiful and happy meeting of the minds and hearts. Alas Reigna hadn't expected it but was indeed happy about it either way and she'd protect him eternally and hadn't ever since then experienced such joy in all her young 700 years of life. Vega Leo Eros had been a very refined man although he had been 350 years Reigna's junior and that had been enough to make her want to protect him.

His eyes were a rare shade of midnight blue and his platinum blonde hair had mesmerized Reigna at first glance as she had never since then seen a man who was quite so elegant. His long blonde hair had been tied back into a long and sleek ponytail. Alas she'd known that she had come to want more than her own life in the most extreme even her own magic had grown more powerful with every spell and every glance she took at her new betrothed. She had grown to care for him more than the air she breathed and somehow that was enough for her to grasp onto.

Although Reigna had been a young and naïve woman, she had loved him with a heart of gold and the disposition of an angel or at least a true goddess of Greek Mythology. Regina had been a most short tempered woman but alas she had been a doting mother of two daughters as well, Reigna had been more than capable as a young woman but the fact that she'd been a defensive lady even though she'd never tried to use her powers for such things. But alas just because she had never used her powers for such a thing doesn't mean that she isn't willing to give her best to protect Vega, her new lover and now betrothed as well.

Vega had loved Reigna as a Priestess of the Temple of Poseidon and a healer due to the fact that her powers were considerably stronger than the typical healer's. She even had the ability to hold strong her faith in Poseidon Greek god of the seas; whom she had always loved. But love for Vega was more than anyone could ever imagine. Even though Vega had always been a rather strong Atlantean male, he was very respectful towards Reigna, who defends those whom she loves and cares about greatly. Reigna had accepted him whole heartedly even though her witchcraft was designed to protect and defend those whom she had loved and truly respected more than words could bring to light.

Reigna had known that she'd been a gifted woman with premonitions and healing abilities too. She had also known that Atlanteans had lived long luxurious lives under the watchful eyes of Poseidon and his son Atlas.

Reigna vowed not to lay waste to the Atlantean race since it was Poseidon who had bestowed upon her such gifts. She had never wanted to be away from Vega for any reason. Reigna had loved Vega and his high and mighty ways though she had known it to be a totally sinful way of living in her mind. It wasn't right for it to be that way even if he hadn't thought it was fine, as long as it didn't go to his head, much less if it ended up forsaking Poseidon and Atlas, their gods, who had given rise to their home Atlantis.

Reigna had everything she'd ever wanted and her love for Vega had grown ever stronger in the summer heat of the Atlantic Ocean where she'd gone swimming all her life. She had never sought a better life than the one she was granted from Poseidon himself. As she had reached her 700th year, she was granted the life of a High Priestess of Poseidon's Temple. It was something that only she could do. After all, she had the strongest faith of anyone that could have assumed the role of High Priestess.

She had foreseen the fate of the many, as though to see where all their destinies would sooner lie, at the end of the Atlanteans, at the end of Atlantis. Vega and his brother Scorpius had been close. But compared to Vega, Scorpius had been a fool and an idiot by Vega's standards. Scorpius had used magic for everyday use. Ultimately taking for granted, the home they had and Poseidon and his son Atlas as well.

This is The Golden Age of Atlantis.

Chapter One ~ The Golden Age

Reigna had not wavered in the faith of the Greek God of the sea, Poseidon who had laid upon her blessing after blessing from three gorgeous nieces and a loving sister also a devoted brother-in-law who had done exactly what Poseidon had wanted of him down to the final letter without question; and never gave away much of himself in an attempt to protect his family and closest friends who had been nearest to him for millennia.

Reigna had planned a formal wedding to her endeared Vega who was 350 years her junior, yet he wanted the wedding even more than his Reigna who had entrusted him to her heart and never wavered in loving him most of all. Vega was all the earthly beauty who had meant so much to her. All the while the love they had shared had been a perpetually unbreakable bond also a god-sent sign, of unyielding devotion in all things connected to the heavens and earth. Somehow that alone was enough to keep her tied to him and his pure heart which had never once been tainted by things unblessed by the gods they worshipped above all things else on earth.

Knowing full well that if they did something that didn't please the gods The Atlantean race would pay the ultimate price in accordance with the broken taboo sin that would warrant such a fitting punishment from Zeus, Poseidon themselves. It would be a price to pay for all of Atlantis to suffer; This is what kept them together as a devoted couple who were quite chaste in all things and refrained from any sensuality and remained strong as a reminder of who keeps them alive and whose lives were in Poseidon's hands at such a time as thus.

Vega had been a devoted Atlantean from a young age of 300 years and he hadn't wavered since and he knew that his Reigna could protect him from sin and love him still. She had done this and so much more her heart and devotions had been a part of him from the day he had fallen in love with her sparkling blue eyes and her pale blonde hair which had been left to flow just above her slender ankles decorated in slender golden straps crisscrossing across her ankles up to her calves which were equally slender and well toned for a female.

Vega had pale blonde hair and gleaming midnight blue eyes which were full of wonder and mystery but of course a very loving man, indeed who had been devoted to his beloved Reigna who had tended the Temple of Poseidon. Reigna's sister Karrina and her family built their home at the foot of Mount Atlas, a volcano that wasn't active as far as anyone had known. But alas that was where Poseidon had ordered Delphus to build their home and their thriving life, love, and truly lavish life style which Reigna herself had. Poseidon had gifted Reigna with the ability to see the future yet to come. If things hadn't changed by the time her visions came to her to foretell the future the Atlanteans surely wouldn't last another century. It was a gift that was passed on to her from her grandmother. Because of that gift she and Vega had been seen as two of Poseidon's own children, though he himself had many, they were the cherished ones as they carried deep within themselves the blood of Poseidon god of the seas the father of Atlantis. They had paid homage to Poseidon daily and nightly Vega and the love of her family and friends who all had the same practices as she had led Atlantis to a fruitful Spring, Summer, Autumn, and Winter as well. Reigna had been gifted with premonitions which she had inherited; from her grandmother on her father's side whom she'd been quite close to since childhood.

Reigna had loved her sister Karrina with all her own existence and prayed daily for her and Valeo also for their three daughters, Vaina, Avianna, and Arianna, who were so beautiful and gifted that even their father Valeo was doting on all three of them and their mother Karrina was so dedicated to her family that nothing else seemed to matter.

Even when things weren't going well with the naval port wanting to rule alone and decimate the temples which were to the gods Poseidon and his son Atlas, Reigna performed a ritual of protection over the two temples which were to be destroyed over time and soon after thus the naval ports soon backed away leaving both temples in peace. Reigna and Vega were happy just to be guarding the same temple together under one roof which her father had arranged for and while Reigna had been truly happy in the union process which had been given Reigna's and Vega's full attention while they had focused their healing powers together to bind one to the heart of the other and asked Poseidon to bless them in their happy union of love and devotion.

It all seemed to be going as planned but there were people who were not quite as enthusiastic about Reigna and Vega. Vega for the most part had been rumored to be the Atlantean bad boy. Soon the news was out about Reigna and Vega being together in an energy binding ceremony which had taken much time and dedication over time; they had gone over to the Kings of Atlantis alas the star-crossed lovers and talented gifted healers of the Golden Age of Atlantis.

Chapter Two ~ A Fate Decided

Reigna had always been one to chant different protective incantations that had been taught to her by her father as she had been born a witch whose bloodline was still stronger than death. The incantations held sacred words that were in their own way very personal to her and her bloodline also. Vega had been there for Reigna all the while during such times as these, where trials of his judgment of where he had come from, as if it hadn't truly mattered even when it reflects what sort of family she'd soon give rise to in the end. Reigna didn't just smolder over the unjust treatment of Vega but her temper pushed her into an intense prayer session with Poseidon and relentlessly to Poseidon she did pray to clear Vega's name. It was a more merciful act than anyone could ever imagine. Poseidon washing Vega in the purifying waters of his own judgment and left his own mark upon Vega's brow; a mark of his own approval which only a divine being could leave behind.

Reigna had been quite impressed with the Prayers which were answered by no less than Poseidon himself. As a result justice had been served and Poseidon had made certain that Vega wouldn't be harmed by his own people who had laid false claims against him. The mark of Poseidon had been placed there in a clear golden blaze which no one could ever explain even if they had tried to do so. Vega being kept alive by Poseidon was indeed all that he could hope for at the very least, it was better than just a good thing it was a sign for other Atlanteans to cease their judgment on Vega. Reigna had taken Vega to their home on the southern shore, where they'd be receiving a splendid view of the sunrise and sunset and it'll be a home to them for centuries to come. At least that is what it was supposed to be for them.

Reigna had embraced Vega and kissed him passionately and placed her hands upon his lower back, which caused him to tremble under her touch it was more than just enchanting. It was a love that would surely surpass time and space it was a love that would conquer death if that is what Poseidon wishes. Reigna knew little of how she could best aid her beloved's desire for her though Poseidon's law had still prevailed at this time.

It was time for her to dedicate herself more than ever to protect that law which had kept them chaste and still wanting one another as much as they had. It was indeed time for them to rededicate themselves to protecting the Temple of Poseidon. Poseidon and Atlas had ruled the Atlantean race with a kind but strict nature. They were not allowed to break even a single law without Poseidon's or Atlas' blessing first, but alas it was Reigna who had every right to defend the

Temple of Poseidon whether it be in blood or in the waters of the sea.

Vega had wanted Reigna with all the life force left in his body and it seemed as though his world would never again be the same as it once was, even when death could be his undoing but again Reigna was always at his side to make things right. It was more than anything that Reigna could ever want, a genuine dream come true for her to see Poseidon bless her passion for her love, but again she was not allowed to break the law that was written in absolution.

It was Vega who had been there for Reigna in all her duties and even with her Premonitions telling her what the future held for her and her people it was more than just fate it was Poseidon's will, which would surely come to be as plainly as if she wanting this with all her own strength. Poseidon had guided her by her heart to clean the Temple and Polish the golden trident upon the altar and the bronze statues of Poseidon as well. It seemed to be more than enough to keep the peace among the Atlanteans and the Gods too. But Reigna had given her best with the premonitions lasting for what seemed to be hours.

She had remained vigilant in her duties and allowed nothing to distract her. Vega had supported her so strongly that even the other Atlanteans were impressed with his abilities to assist his lady fiancé; who had kept worshipping Poseidon night and day and praying for her people to be left in peace after so many wars with the Athenians. It was a wonder any of the men had survived at all; it was Reigna who had tended to the wounded and the dying of her race as any other healer wasn't cut out for the job to tend the half dead and the dying. Among them were the naval officers who had pleaded with Reigna to see them as her patients and were concerned with staying alive and seeing their families again. It was Reigna who had tended them with a simple touch to their wounds. She would heal them with the sacred prayers to Poseidon to keep them alive. It was almost too much with the premonitions she bore within her she pleaded with the captain of the naval officers to cease the fighting. It wasn't fair for all this to happen and force her to heal all the wounded and tend the dying.

It was Reigna who was to be thanked for the recovery of the many. Vega was stunned as he was forced to watch Reigna reveal her gifts of healing to him and the precious fact that she was the strongest Atlantean healer they had to take care of them. She was a kind and nurturing woman in the lightness of her gift of healing; she was truly a sight to behold as she took care of everyone who was wounded and on the verge of dying. It was enough for him to love her more and more with every passing moment she spent healing the masses alone it was her privilege to do so. Reigna finished up for the day with healing the wounded and dying, she had given Vega a well placed kiss upon his lips and let up immediately before things got too heated at the Temple of Poseidon. Vega had gently embraced Reigna in his strong well toned arms that had defended her honor from his wretched elder brother who had called her a witch, a fiend, in Atlantean skins. It wasn't fair that he had done her multiple injustices all at once.

Reigna may be the daughter of a witch and have witch's blood in her veins but her powers were strictly used to help others and not herself. It was a power she used for the good of others, that is and was always to be the absolute truth and nothing less. It was Reigna who had decided that it was a wise decision for her to use her powers to help protect her people and the Temples of Poseidon and Atlas. It was the only way she could assure their safety; it was, though, the most powerful magic of her time of blood sacrifice from her own veins.

Vega knew what it was to love a born white witch but although it might have been a blessing from Poseidon for this to be sure Vega had to do his part and take care of her and comfort her through her grievances,

Alas Reigna had to do her part and protect her people from themselves and their greediness which could and quite possibly would destroy them all. It wasn't fair to Vega that this could cost his Reigna her blood if only she could protect her people. It was all foretold later that night at the later service in paying homage to Poseidon their god of the seas that if their current actions continued the way they have been they will all meet a watery grave of fire and lava with no hope of survival unless they can change their ways.

It was Vega who had stood upon the Altar of Poseidon with a chalice of the waters of the Atlantic Ocean in his hands reflecting their fates. If they hadn't believed Reigna's words alone it was their own decisions of what would come of their futures, if they kept rejecting the words of Poseidon and Lady Reigna's as well but alas every fate reflected was done so in disaster that could kill them all if it was allowed to go on like this. Vega had done all in his power to convince his brethren to listen to Reigna, for her prophesies had never failed to come to fruition and warn her people, and this time was no different. It was all that Vega knew of Reigna that could change the course of history for them all as if she had to reveal all that she had seen to her parents in due time.

But alas it was enough time still for her to prepare for the worst scenario to come into existence that is for their brethren will bring upon them all, the only way to avert this disaster was to use their blood to pay homage to Poseidon, using blood sacrifice. Reigna's Grandmother - Celestia Marcial Valera knew too well what was to come and bring an end to their race. It was blood that must be spilled in a basin upon the altar of Poseidon if they were likely live the coming cataclysmic day that will likely be their last days alive on earth and by the blood of witchcraft that had flowed through Reigna's veins that had brought forth the destiny of their dying day and night unless migration might take place their lives will indeed end.

Make no mistake, anything they might do will have to be in blood whether it is a blood sacrifice which we each slice open our hands or wrists with the sacred dagger of Poseidon and allow the blood to flow into the basin which sits upon the altar of Poseidon. This would be their last hope; Vega knew where they were going to be if the gods made their choice now. It was too much and therefore he had gone to his family and told them of the prophesy made by lovely Reigna; who had been a fair reminder of the father of the Atlanteans. It wasn't fair that the Atlanteans were becoming less fearful of the gods and a more self centered and greedy.

It wasn't enough for all this to come to pass; it was all for the sake of their survival it must be said unto them the Eros Family must know the truth of the prophesy foretold earlier that day. Karrina had to see what her sister had seen through the basin of Atlas it was her magic that allowed her to see it also. Valeo had to know that the first of the disasters would happen right on top of them. It was the best that could be said at that point for their daughters' sake it was too much to bear for Valeo and somehow he knew that death was imminent now that the damage had been done by their own people who became too greedy and self centered. They ceased their worship of Poseidon and his son Atlas. It was going to be a massacre if nothing would be done about this soon and Valeo had known it too. Their lives were on the line and it was like the end of the world coming after so long, it was as if even their gods had forsaken them to their sensualistic wiles.

It was too much to ask of any Atlantean but it was necessary for their survival; they had gone later that night to see Reigna, who had seen this first in the form of premonitions and nightmares, which were given to her by the gods. It was all a matter of time until it all fell apart in front of the Temple of Poseidon to have them each blessed with their bloodline being of descent of a witch daughter of Poseidon, and with their powers, they were blessed until the day of the calamity due to befall their race. It was all Reigna could do as the High Priestess of the Temple of Poseidon. It was all just a matter of time until the gods decided to do away with them all leaving behind a prophesy unlike the one foretold by Reigna but by the gods themselves. Vega had held on to each of Reigna's nieces as they were blessed by Reigna, the only woman he'd ever loved. It was enough at that point. It was all a fanciful time for each of them. It was to end all too soon; but again Reigna had given her all for her family's good.

Chapter Three ~ Fated To Be ...

Reigna had rallied on, her family together, to try to stabilize their futures and keep the homage going to Poseidon. It all seemed so futile as her people stopped attending the Temple's service. It just didn't improve by the next two crescent moons and it became obvious what had to be done and Vega had seen to the provisions needed at this time. The seas didn't seem as peaceful as they normally had been which meant that Poseidon had been most displeased with their race. It just didn't seem right for all this to happen to them. It was so unfair, so unjust, that the Atlanteans had to suffer for not paying their dues to the ones who had given them a bountiful harvest, short winters and hot summers with their children, and junior members of each of the Temples.

Vega had fetched the water for the ceremony to take place the following night. Reigna knew too well what might happen if any of this went unchecked. It was Poseidon who had guided her actions and lent her his strength to wield his mighty trident. When the continent was in turmoil, it wasn't fair to her that her race had to suffer for a few misgivings over time. But even if that had been the case, she couldn't let go of the fact that she had to fight off her own people, due to their own set of separate beliefs; it was set now. The end was set in stone. Alas, the Valera and Eros Families had come together to shed their blood upon the altar of Poseidon. Into the basin of blood had they sliced their wrists and cut open their hands it seemed more fitting that even the children of the family had shown a little contribution for their beliefs. They too took the dagger to cut open their hands and wrists to keep their families safe and know that Poseidon will not destroy them. Their own innocence had become a chant from the families and closest and most trusted friends, for they knew that Poseidon would not forgive anyone who thinks only of himself or herself.

Reigna was among the first to spill her blood upon the altar and allowed it to flow freely into the basin that was already filled with the waters of the Atlantic Sea as tribute to Poseidon. Her father Regulous had been next, then Regina who hadn't originally believed her youngest daughter and her premonitions. Until all the signs were there and pointing to the gods angry wrath, coming to crash down atop the entire Atlantean race, Reigna had known the answers to what needed to be done. At this point, it was all due to their people's ignorance and unknowingly doing forbidden acts, above all things and that was in league with acting selfishly and ceasing all worship of Poseidon and his son Atlas. It wasn't enough they had become such sensual beings that it became a forbidden act, as selfishness was above all things a taboo, a sin that wasn't supposed to have been broken … ever. She had given her best to Vega whom she had loved;

and out of sheer concern, she had taken hold of Vega's hand, looked him deep in his midnight blue eyes for the answer of an unspoken question and he nodded so as to give Reigna the answer to her prayer.

She had smiled at him with the dagger in her right hand, his hand in her left hand; she slit open his wrist with perfect precision. She gave him a long and passionate kiss upon the altar as the blood flowed freely into the basin that had been partially filled with the waters of the Atlantic Ocean, the domain of Poseidon. The basin was filled almost to the top with the blood of these noble Atlanteans who had voluntarily bled themselves into the basin, that was filled with Atlantean blood from those worthy enough to be claimed as the most pure of the race; alas it wasn't enough to merely be cleansed by the sea, but now it was to be the best sacrifice left done by Reigna, Vega, and their families as well.

She allowed the blood of her family and lover to flow freely into the basin although there was one man who hadn't shown up at the ceremony that was Scorpius, Vega's elder brother, who had scoffed at Reigna's abilities as High Priestess from the very start. It was a doomed story from there on, it wasn't supposed to be like this. They all knew that they would all be ended in blood, eventually. They had all known that blood is the only sacrifice for their sins that can possibly atone for their crimes of ceasing worship of the gods. It is only fair as retribution for going through so much change at once. But alas, Reigna chanted a spell to activate their blood's magical qualities. Eventually they all followed in the chant which sounded more like Gregorian Chants in an ancient language which had long since been used by Atlantean witches or those of magical heritage. It seemed their blood started to shine gold in the basin which sat upon the altar. The Pillar of Poseidon started to shine gold along with their blood that was being Sacrificed for the good of their people, it was all for the good of them. It seemed so full of promise and prosperous ideals; much like those they had when Atlantis was new. But now it seemed as if their people had become too self important and stopped looking to the gods for their crops and their sensual desires had over taken their day to day lives.

***

Poseidon's and Atlas' displeasure of this sinful world they had given rise to couldn't possibly be so foolish, at least that is what they had thought at first, that they knew the risks of letting this go unpunished.

Zeus was already angry at the Atlanteans for their disregard of the laws put forth from the beginning of what was to be seen as the Age of Aquarius. It was a dire time for the Atlanteans. Reigna tried all her strongest magic to save them from the wrath; but alas it was to be the end of days for the Atlanteans in a fortnight. Later that night they had left the Temple of Poseidon and went on with their lives it was all too much for the gods to see. Reigna had resumed her life at home with her Vega and they sat together nestled together on her lavish sofa which faced the starry sky. The full moon was peeking through the tree tops which added to the serene of their home. They had found in each other's arms a home they could call their own. It was time to do the right thing and settle for a cup of tea to bond over. It was a fine Atlantean blend which had grown wildly in the mountains of Atlantis, but now, it seemed as if their happiness was being taken away. All because of their people who hadn't adhered to the gods, when things were starting to get desperate for their survival it was only for their own good that at this point it wasn't going to be long until the end came upon them; it was the first night since the ceremony and the sense of great unease filled the air. Vega pulled Reigna to his heart which was a strong heartbeat, quite unlike anything she's ever felt before. It was truly a miracle that they were allowed to stay to together until the end.

***

"Poseidon and his mercy, grant thy strength to endure your wrath until the end of days to come upon us from your mighty place in high Mount Olympus in Greece" was the sacred prayer whispered between Reigna and Vega as they held each other close. In the darkness of night, in the parlor lit by the light of the full moon, a brilliance unlike anything ever seen before, Reigna embraced Vega with much love as he had held her close to his heart. It was more passionate than all the nights they had spent together. Time and again, it had become the night of nights as his arms held her tight. Her trembling just wouldn't stop. It was the only answer he could give her to stop her trembling; it was his arms that calmed her when nothing else could. It was Vega who had given up so much of his blood that he was weakened too and leaned on his lovely bride to be. She, being a healer, couldn't allow his weakness to persist much longer or else it could cause him to die in pain. It wasn't enough she had to become their high Priestess and their healer. Now she has to be her people's salvation too. Now that just isn't fair. The curses are final, the laws and commandments are absolute and now it seems that justice had been done in the god's mind. The next day was treated as one of their last days alive but their chastity remained in place and it would mean they wouldn't have sex until their dying day. It was the only way they could give thanks to Poseidon for their most amazing lives which they had lived to the fullest; the only gift they could give to Poseidon and Atlas was their chastity and nothing more was fitting as they went to the Temple of Poseidon with its daily cleansings and windows blessed and cleansed as well. It had become the cleanest of the Temples in all of Atlantis.

Soon they had the altar arranged with flowers of all sorts and inlaid with white roses and blue bells. It was the most elaborate arrangement they could do together, their last act as a couple that would be performed in the Temple of Poseidon. Their lasting kiss that day was as beautiful as the Temple though it was chaste it was one of beauty and it seemed so natural too it was indeed too natural and when they realized this they pulled away out of fear of the gods wrath. The gods were angry enough already. But alas Reigna had taken hold of Vega's hand with her right hand and with her left caressed his chest just over his heart that started to race as she gave him her best smile.

***

Soon she had to let go of him due to her faltering resolve as High Priestess. It had become too irresistible to not want more than to be in his presence; it was all so unfair and yet they were still unmarried and they needed that marriage to fulfill each other all the same. It was a fate that they didn't want but within the next two days and two nights it would all be over; they will suffer no more the insufferable agony of remaining virgins. It's not going to end in marriage said the melancholy Reigna; instead it'll end in blood and death and there will be no stopping the gods now. It's too late for that. Vega gave no answer but an arm around his maiden love who had endured losing him in dreams and premonitions alike. But alas, it'll happen just as she said and he could feel it himself just how hopeless their situation is. He placed his hands on her shoulders and pulled her close to his chest once more it was their last known embrace before judgment day of their race. It was meant to be a sign of their eternal embrace in the next life. It was a sacred moment between lovers that was to take place between them. Vega had laid his right hand upon his lover's right hip where her priestess robes were gathered into a series of pleats and

23

sashes which were as elaborate as the Temple of Poseidon was. It was then time to pack up their supplies and head home for the night after a twelve hour service to Poseidon, who had given her warning upon warning about the path that her people were going to take her down if this didn't cease. The floral sacrifice had given them one fortnight to give them an extra day and night to prepare themselves for the worst.

***

Grandmother Celestia had already migrated the day before the service with a few other faithful followers of Poseidon those who were fearful of the gods. Scorpius came one day to pay a much needed visit to Reigna and his brother Vega to repent his idiocy and selfish greed as well as his power-hungry nature. She was stunned that the pig-headedness had faded but the recklessness of his nature had not done him any favors much less earned him any merit from Poseidon or Atlas. It just wasn't right that his crimes have been forgiven regardless of the house visit to reconcile the fact that they're blood relatives. But this was very uncharacteristic of Scorpius as his reputation was that of a lady's man and magic-using fool. Reigna knew a lot of things about Scorpius and one of those things was the fact that he wouldn't stoop to repenting for his many crimes against his brother's honor or the honor of Poseidon and thinking himself higher than the gods who were going to be the downfall.

Vega knew his brother wouldn't be so stupid as to go so far as repentance when that would simply get Scorpius killed in a matter of moments. It wouldn't be enough to just say that he was sorry. Reigna placed her kind hand upon Scorpius' heart to sense if the man within was still there. If so, she would have to kill him by her own hand. It was her duty as the High Priestess of the Temple of Poseidon; she knew that her love couldn't watch the death of his elder brother. Vega retreated to the prayer room within their home to pray to Poseidon and the other gods for a swift end. It wasn't enough at this point, Tears were stinging the corners of his midnight blue eyes and as he reached the prayer room tears began to fall, a sign that it was nearly over, and the end was drawing ever closer to them.

Reigna had tested the virtues as Vega had been upstairs praying to the gods for their mercy and it seemed as if all hope was gone. But again Scorpius was a most unpleasant Atlantean indeed, he knew that his brother wouldn't survive the encounter with Reigna who had been most bothered by the odd behavior. This left Vega at odds with his brother even more than before. It was all a matter until the truth was revealed and either it could end in Scorpius' redemption or worse that his death which would easily be done in blood. It was a risk that needed to be taken after all this time as it was Vega's blood that he'd been out for and it was known that it wouldn't be long until Scorpius lost his own life for retribution after making a mockery of the gods and their wrath that would soon be brought upon their race.

Vega stayed in the prayer room and prayed to all the gods who seemed so angry with them as it was already. He could no longer contain his tears. He may end up losing his elder brother first. He knew the price for disobeying the gods and it was going to cost them all their lives and their homeland as well. "It will rise again." That is what he had heard whispered in his ear.

As he was praying he heard Athena, Goddess of Wisdom: "Atlantis will rise again all in due time. It will happen." Vega's tears fell in silence.

Athena continued, "My dearly beloved Vega it is not of my wishes but the gods' who wanted me to do this deed as the last act of salvation for our race. It was not the way I wanted it to be. I had no desire for bloodshed in my home, our home. It was supposed to be a place of love and harmony too. This wasn't supposed to be a house of bloodshed. It was supposed to be a house of love and compassion, honesty and peace too."

Reigna added "I never wanted this to conspire here in this house it's not right for this to happen that I lose my brother-in-law and you lose your brother. I am most aggravated by this turn of events. It's not right that families be torn asunder by this. I cannot say just what your tears do to me my dear sweet Vega. It's time we face the facts that

Atlantis is going to meet its watery and fiery end. Make no mistake about that Vega. It's time. I knew that we would not be able to avert the god's wrath now, but alas, we tried so hard to do just that in whatever way we could but it was all pointless in the end."

I know Reigna, "Let's just sit like this a while longer and enjoy the stillness of the evening. It's time we just take in each moment we have left together."

"Yes Vega it's time we just sit here in the silence of our home. As the evening approaches let us prepare our evening feast with the family before the end comes ever nearer? I agree Vega. Let us go and have supper with the rest of the family it's only proper after what just happened. I mean I didn't expect that brother of yours to pay us such an accursed visit and certainly didn't expect him to take the blade, from my hand and kill himself as repentance. It wasn't supposed to go like this; it wasn't supposed to start here, though it did indeed start here in our loving home. It will hereby be cursed by the gods and it was time to accept that blood is what's going to flow from the mountain tops. We'll die amidst all of it. Indeed, it's the one thing that was forbidden by the gods, to kill out of fellowship; not a suicide that your brother committed right in front of me and out of shame for his actions prior to this night," said Reigna.

Vega continued, "It was a suicide worthy of such befitting crimes and until now, I felt ashamed to have Scorpius as my elder brother. He did nothing but want me dead for the sake of having the High Priestess and white witch bride, who is so loved by the gods and a woman whom I love so much even without his blessings," said Vega who was now drying his tears after losing his irritating elder brother.

Vega and Reigna got ready to go to her family's home on the outermost part of Atlantis and she took hold of her beloved's hand, gave her a smile and squeezed her hand comfortingly. He and Reigna left their home and went on their way to Reigna's and Korrina's parents' home to make supper and spend time with the family. It was gift enough for them to have a family supper for the last time before the day of blood and fire which was to put an end to them all. It was a joyous time where they could laugh and focus on the company of their children, grandchildren, and the gods' bounty which had then been laid before them upon their fanciful table; it wasn't right for any of this to end.

"I know that I may be speaking out of turn, Father, but being a High Priestess has been such a rewarding experience and helping so many people had become my life's mission to make sure that everyone lives a pure and happy life without the curses of sins committed by our brethren. It shouldn't fall upon us to pay for their sinful ways," said a resolute Reigna, on the verge of tears over losing what maybe left of her home.

"Calm down, we have children in our midst. They shouldn't have to hear this from you; not now, not when it's this close to the end of the end of the world, as we know it. Is that clear Reigna?"

"Yes Karrina. It's as clear as the great quartz crystal that gives us our power."

"That's my proud sister," said a very proud and resolute Karrina.

Vega comforted Reigna and it was the night of making merry with the bountiful goods set before them, upon the family dining table.

Chapter Four ~ To The End

The rest of the meal was spent with the family laughing and hoping for the best future they could get even if it's not on Atlantis. It was a fated destruction that they all knew was coming; it was only a matter of time.

"Thank you for the meal mother and father," said Reigna and Vega who were now ready to die for whatever had come to be thought of them by the gods, who were now passing judgment on them all. It was now or never. They returned home and collapsed into each other's arms as they cried together knowing the end was indeed drawing near for them all. It was an unfair justice that they themselves hadn't deserved and had known this all along too. Alas it wasn't a fairness that could be justified by their deaths and the deaths of all those whom had been held most dear from the children to their parents.

"It wasn't supposed to go this way; at least now we know the truth of what is about to happen to us when it's time for us to face the gods' wrath," Reigna said through tears stinging her blue eyes. She could no longer put on a brave front for Vega. It was alright that they both ended up crying that night as they held onto each other knowing that their wedding would never have the chance to take place amongst their family and friends.

The following day was sunny. But it was colder than usual. It was as if death was trying to kill them himself. It could've been done by Hades' own hand. But alas, it was impossible. "There would be no way Hades would intervene in this sorry state we're in now." Later on that day Regina, covered in volcanic ash and in tears, had come to Reigna's and Vega's home.

Regina told them, "Karrina and the children, also Valeo they're… all gone… they died in the volcano eruption just three hours ago. The oldest of the girls slowed the lava for their parents who were carrying Arianna to safety. But in the end they all perished within the hour."

It was a fate that devastated both Reigna and Vega. It was worse still trying to keep themselves from falling apart at the seams into a sea of tears of sorrow. It wasn't enough to merely cry. Reigna shut down and loved only Vega, begging the gods not to take him too. It only made things worse now. It was a fortnight that day and it was bound to end that very day. The gods had written their warnings across her dreams and Vega couldn't do much but stay strong for her and he held her tighter and tighter reassuring her that, if he dies, she'd not be too far behind him. It was a bitter sweet moment for the star-crossed lovers as they prepared to meet their end for the sake of the new world to come into existence after their passing.

Vega had soothed her until the panic died down, the only thing that could be done at that point. It was their helplessness that proved that the gods have always had the upper hand in their fates. As far as their fates are concerned, the gods are bound to destroy them on the promised day of their end. It was a day that would mark the end of the Atlantean empire. It was a new era and they had all known that the price for their sins was death of all their race and all their brethren would suffer greatly for the sins of their kind. The story that would be recited throughout history and they all knew it. Reigna foretold the gods' prophesy that was told to Vega, that the apparent goddess Athena, the goddess of wisdom and strategy, was then made true.

Later that day they went to the Temple of Poseidon polished the statue of Poseidon, and cleaned the stained glass windows. The chandelier was hanging as beautifully as it always had. She cleaned and polished the altar and the floor around it until it was spotless. The very knowing that it was their last day alive made these deeds seem bittersweet. It wasn't until noon of that day until the direness of their situation really took hold. It was more than just the children's deaths that struck home for Reigna as her mother. Regina was caught by the lava flow from earlier that day. It was too much for the beautiful, but now grieving, Reigna. It was time for solemnity for those who were still alive and those who served under her as handmaidens of Atlas. Atlas, the first king of Atlantis, was most bitter since it was her family dying off first after taking the life of Scorpius, Vega's idiotic and foolish elder brother. Though Scorpius killed himself, he left Reigna feeling responsible for his killing himself.

Vega was cleaning the windows and making repairs to whatever cracks there were in the glass and Reigna was tending the floral arrangements. They were stealing glances at one another from across the isles while working their hardest so that when it would sink in, it would at least go down looking its best even though there'd not be one soul to see it. At least the gods would be pleased. All the while to spite what their brethren would believe that the gods would sink this Temple beneath the waves, she kept her love alive in her heart even though it wouldn't last too much longer. Because just as Vega was finishing up the repairs to the windows inspecting every little detail in them, a violent earthquake shook the Temple of Poseidon down to its foundations. The chandelier rattled unnervingly as Reigna rushed over to Vega. His midnight blue eyes widened as a shatter was heard then… blood poured from his chest. His heart had been pierced and Reigna knew that she might not be able to save him; but she was willing to try to heal him. Though her tears were now flowing freely down her pale cheeks, she wouldn't accept this to be the way they die.

She was across the aisle from her beloved Vega and before she could reach him he gave her a smile which could've easily been his way of saying that they'll meet again on the other side. She didn't want to accept that and before she could reach him to heal him, before she could scream, the chandelier had fallen loose from the fastenings that kept it securely held to the ceiling. By a violent tremor that landed it upon beautiful Reigna's head, Vega died soon after and together they died that day. It was the day of reckoning and everyone had known this and now their beautiful High Priestess and their white witch had died in a pool of crimson red blood. Vega's blood mingled with Reigna's.

It was the end of the era, the end of their world to make way for the new world to be made and created to be one of perfect harmony and less corrupted. Time will tell just how much like Atlantis it would too soon become. Vega's mother and father and Reigna's father Regulous had found the Temple of Poseidon in shambles and the lovers in one pool of blood only separated by what was left to be the statue of Poseidon. The parents of these star-crossed lovers could do nothing but grieve over the deaths of their dearest children and their only hope now … dead. It was too late now to save either of them. The end had come just as she foretold but upon the altar she inscribed one last prophesy for her people, "The Greatness of the Land of Atlantis will rise again by the power of the Almighty Gods and their powers to make us real once again."

This prophesy left her father in disbelief and Vega's parents in awe of what could be their last hope for salvation from the gods. But again it was short lived as they left the Temple with their beloved children another violent earthquake shook the ground beneath their feet and they fell to the ground with their beloved children. And the High Priestess' rose quartz gone inside the crystal itself. The Priestess' love, Vega, had an emerald crystal hanging around his neck and their crystals together protected their parents and family. It was a bond made in blood after the ceremony had taken place several days before all this destruction and death had taken place. In a way it was insurance that even if they should die their remaining relatives would not go down right away as Reigna had wanted the families to hold out for as long as possible even when their spirits had passed on.

Regulous was convinced that they still had a fighting chance to live this day let come what may. It wasn't supposed to be this way but indeed a way that the blood that still flowed from his youngest daughter's head formed another prophesy that said, "Blood will flow in oceans into rivers and make way for the coming of a new era where the Atlantean race will be no more than legends and rumors until the day *ATLANTIS WILL RISE AGAIN FROM THE SEAS* and a ghost continent will it so be called as the dead will not be buried." Regulous was in disbelief that his daughter would receive such a message from the gods and goddesses.

The body of his dear Reigna, his youngest daughter, dead in his arms covered in blood was still as beautiful as she'd always been. The wound upon her head being a horrific sight as it was, didn't do anything but cause him to want to bury his beloved daughter with the man that was soon to be husband; Regulous had asked this of Vega's parents and Felicia had nodded in truest approval and Daemion had followed suit. They agreed that Reigna and Vega should be buried by the shore line of where the incoming tsunami was about to take place. Before it happened they were buried together in the white sands of Atlantis by the south shore of the mainland. It was as if they were sleeping together covered in each other's blood and embracing in a loving scene that would have left the memory in a vivid color through the Parent's last dying moments.

It was too much for Regulous to lose first his eldest daughter and his son-in-law and his three gifted granddaughters all at once, then his wife and the mother of the family whom he'd loved since childhood. He then took his own life by sitting by the grave of the two people who could've carried on the race through their bloodlines as the tsunami came and destroyed everything in sight killing Regulous, Daemion, and Felicia all at that exact moment, leaving their imprints upon the grave site of the lovers.

After that day there was little left of the famed Atlantis as both Temples now slept beneath the waves of the Atlantic Ocean. Alas the remains of the sleeping lovers had long since been forgotten and no one remembered them and all their sacrifices as the prophesies died then and hope ultimately seemed gone. Celestia Valera migrated safely to Egypt to live out the rest of her life grieving the loss of her family and even her beautiful youngest grand daughter's death had reached the shores of Egypt.

The prophesies had visited Celestia on the morn of their last day alive it wasn't fair that they die before having their own children. Knowing this made Celestia most aggravated of the fact that they were unfairly judged and the same day the loving couple were martyred as sacrifices of the land of what used to be their Atlantis, Greek for the daughter of Atlas. It was written that Atlantis will one day rise from the sea floor. Celestia knew that none of this could bring back the dead dearly beloved. It was only a stipulation for the dead; it wasn't enough to merely know that Reigna and Vega can rest in peace.

Though losing her son was the most devastating news she'd received as her last living relatives had died one by one she learned the Egyptian ways and their gods and goddesses and served the people by making shawls to shield the women and their children from blowing sand from sandstorms. She immersed herself in knitting and sewing all forms of embroidery to decorate the shawls and make them a pleasant accessory.

The Pharaoh had come to believe well in her capacities for fortune telling and sewing as well as her knitting. Though she was young in appearance she possessed much knowledge on nearly all subjects. He saw her as a great asset to the Egyptians and her people. The gods had clearly blessed her with foresight as well which was well beyond all human perception possible. She knew how much gratitude she'd receive for her gifts and it was more than just a mere gift now it was the only thing she had left after she'd lost her home and her entire family. It was enough to say she'd been among the last of the Atlanteans. It was time she had faced the facts that she's going to have to learn to move on; and go on with her life. She would see the rise and fall of centuries staring into the distance where Atlantis once stood proud.

Chapter Five ~ Dawn of A New Era

It is many eons later in the present day New York City; the year is 2015. My name is Rachel Elise Barnett. It's a beautiful sunny day, and I'm off to work at the renowned diamond company Tiffany's. I'm a sales representative for Tiffany's & Co. and I couldn't ask for a better job. It's social though the guys at work do come across as a rather shady lot. I get my lunch and coffee breaks and it's a fitting life for the likes of me. Though I'm social I would never settle for a shady guy from work; it's just not for me and everyone who knows me and what I'm about know and understand this.

I am just not into shady guys and it bugs me enough when I have to go and scare them off. This is why I don't attend office parties. These shady guys shouldn't have been able to get this sort of high-class job. I know that some may consider me to be rather stuck up but it is their own fault for me acting this way. It's no fault of mine at least not directly; this is just how I have to be. I had shut many men out of my life my father was indeed a proud and strong man. He had encouraged me to chase what it was that I wanted out of life though my mother abandoned us.

My father was as handsome as a prince charming from those childhood fairytales that he used to read to me. As a young girl it was more than that I could see the signs, now written in my life and all its events that had been written in the stars of my fate. It's clear now that my father had known enough about me that I had to take a closer look. Now that I'm older and more understanding of the depth of mankind; no longer am I as shallow as I once was. Though I was brought up Catholic something inside me said that Catholicism isn't my true religion and for a time I thought that voice was correct... But again it wasn't who I was brought up to be. My father might know more about me and this annoying little voice in my head.

I attended to my work like I'd always done, selling the highest quality diamonds and out-doing the men certainly did have its perks. It was as if the goddess Athena herself was guiding me and my decisions from afar. I had done quite a bit better than everyone else and even my best friend Jessica Karen Myers had been impressed with my track record. Each diamond was so well chosen that even my boss Rose Tiffany had been so satisfied with my abilities that she had appointed me to sell the best diamonds to the top celebrities. "Rachel," said Rose, "You've done so well please won't you assist some of our more exclusive clients?"

"Yes I'd be glad to, Rose," replied Rachel with the proper amount of friendliness allowed to someone of her position; it was indeed a chance of a lifetime for Rachel. It was a better chance than any to show the men how it's done, but alas, all they did was fraternize with her. It wouldn't have done them much good anyway all she did was death glare at them. She worked with their more influential clientele giving her the recognition of her skills at picking diamonds for their quality not quantity isn't cutting it.

Jessica had stopped me after work to see if I was still having those bizarre dreams if they could even be called that at any rate … I am.

"Jessica it's starting to disrupt my sleep at night it's insufferable; I really can't stand this any longer I am so worried about my career now that if I keep losing sleep like this I won't be able to stay at the office."

"Oh stop worrying Rachel, and do some research at the library if this talking isn't cutting it."

"Yes Jessica I know and I'll head to the library now to get that research done and though my father is out of town right now I suppose that I can always call him later on when I get desperate enough to solve this mayhem that is my life."

Rachel continues, "I know now that my life isn't going to get any easier if this crap doesn't improve. I mean honestly Jessica I've had enough of this and its hocus pocus which seems to be the case of my dreams at this point, it's clear that this has got to stop and soon at least this is what I hope."

"Well good luck Rachel; I pray that you can find the answers you're looking for today at the library and finally be free of all the ails of those dreams. I know that you'll finally be free from such troublesome dreams that plague your slumber my friend. It is so unfair that you should sacrifice your sleep and your work with it, so please, Rachel, take care of yourself okay? I know that you're dealing with those wretched dreams have to be taking their toll on you now so please Rachel take care and I'll see you tomorrow at work. Alright, Rachel?"

"Yes of course Jessica, see you tomorrow bright and early and I better get going now too, Jess. Bye."

"Yeah. Bye, Rachel. See you tomorrow, bright and early."

Rachel then got into her royal blue Porsche that her father had bought for her when she turned 19. It was beautiful and pristine and hadn't ever had an accident in her years of having it. She was off to the library and she had no major expectations seeing as she'd never done anything like this before. This is the one time she'd ever taken stock into believing in dreams which had somehow come about in such ways as this.

Rachel had known little of her family tree except that her father came from a rather wealthy family not to mention that both her parents came from very old families and now she's making a living on her own selling premium diamonds at Tiffany's & Co. It was now time she uncovers the mysteries behind these dreams. It wasn't merely enough to feel like the outcast of her family. It was well worth just cutting herself off from everyone else except for her father who had defended his little girl and all her decisions too.

Though he was out of town on business, she still gave and received phone calls from him daily. Rachel had given her best to push from her mind the last dream she had until she was certain of what it was. She was never one to give up the ghost without purpose in doing so. Rachel had finally arrived at the library where her research was to take place; she had resolved herself to put from her mind the places and things and focus only on the names which appeared in dreams.

Rachel had worked tirelessly on her research of names that had appeared in her dreams and she stayed at the library for several hours until she found the details she was looking for. She printed every detail she could manage to get until all that remained was to pay for all her labors in finding the answers she could manage to get all at once.

Just as she was gathering her things together she saw this astonishingly good looking tall young man with platinum blonde hair, long to his waist even when it was tied back in a ponytail. His eyes were the shade of midnight blue that was said in legends to be a particularly rare shade of blue, only known to be that of Atlantean origin. But it was only a legend, nothing remains visible of Atlantis. It was time she

pulled herself together and stopped gawking at the tall …
handsome … stranger. She'd felt the attraction to him almost
immediately. It was too much. She'd never been compelled
to get to know a man at least until he turned up and gave her
a pleasant smile that was enough to cause her to go weak in
the knees.

Rachel had gone straight to the counter to pay her
thirty five dollars for her findings and he watched her pull
her papers from the counter and into her library bag. His eyes
locked with hers a second time and she couldn't look away.
His white suit was so professional and left her spellbound
and instantly she knew he was as well off as she herself is
now. At this very moment; she couldn't resist one more look
at him and it seemed that destiny's wheel was turning. It was
now time for Rachel to find love in the eyes of that boy, that
man, who had all the youthful appearance of a movie star.
That didn't fit either because he was just too much of a
temptation for her so she left the library and got into her car.
She slowed her heart rate as it was hammering in her chest so
fast like she'd been jump started by a car charger; the oddest
feeling she had ever experienced in all her life.

***

Rachel turned on the radio and the song *Send Me A
Light* came on and she couldn't resist singing the song as it
played. A vision of a happy couple appeared and their smiles
were so perfect, almost as if they were born to be the
happiest together. It was perfection born in themselves; the

joy of their being together in a summertime romance. That seemed like the best way to describe them, at first, as her voice carried on with the song she saw her mystery man's midnight blue eyes transfixed in her mind. She knew enough of the darkness that did away with the Atlanteans back then it was more than that now. She was back to her time as soon as she'd pulled into her favorite coffee hot spot, just a block from her penthouse suite. It seemed as if she had fallen out of her own skin when the same guy from the library had walked in computer in hand and he took another look at Rachel. She was again unable to look away from the man's blue eyes that pierced the ice cold depths of her heart (that had been left cold by the men who couldn't get close to her).

Rachel looked up from her research papers and couldn't see anything more than blue eyes, beautiful and compassionate. It was more than anything that she had ever felt before; it was more than just a purely kindred spirit, it was her kind eyes that drew him nearer to her. He asked to join her. She didn't refuse him much less turn him away. Her blonde hair now tossed over her right shoulder and sky blue eyes peered up at him through long dark eyelashes. A beautiful conversation came out beautifully and he knew full well what she was going to say to him and he said it before she could say it in a heartbeat.

Rachel turned to her stunningly handsome guest sitting directly across from her. His midnight blue eyes had something so mysterious in them that she couldn't place it, at least not at first. It was something truly beautiful that even the most enigmatic people couldn't be so beautiful. Rachel was almost beside herself with the man before her. He was someone truly special even she could see that it was a more elaborate gift than even she could imagine. It was his gift to be able to break down her defenses and so amazing that he could do this to her with only a glance in her direction.

"What is your name?" asked the stranger with a perfect smile, "My name is Rachel Elise Barnett. I'm a sales representative at Tiffany's & Co. I haven't needed a man to tell me how to live my life; I have my father and that's quite enough for that part of my life. The men at work are nothing, if not awful as they keep staring at me and they hit on me too as well; it's not enough to just be away from them I have to death glare at them just to scare them off; I am sick and tired of having to put up with their antics every day that I go to work."

"I can imagine it's becoming a bit of a bother by now, am I correct, Rachel?" asked the stranger with an elegant smile.

"Well … you're not wrong."

"I see ah, how rude of me for not introducing myself. My name is Noah Mark Levier. It's a pleasure to make your acquaintance, Rachel."

"The pleasure is all mine, Noah, at least you seem smarter than the men I have to work alongside with everyday of the week."

"Thanks Rachel you're too kind, though I'm in a first-rate med school which isn't any easy task to get into at any rate. My mother sees that I get only the best education and my elder brother assists with the studies though he can be a bit callous to women. It's not recommended that you approach him under any circumstance in the slightest. I am close to him yes though he's a far cry from a gentleman like myself. I get this attitude from my mom. And well my father… I just don't want to mention him at all he's more like my elder brother and my mother left my father when we were kids."

Rachel sips her coffee.

Noah continues, "My elder brother has gradually become bitter toward all women because of the matter. But either way Rachel I'm the opposite of my brother. He might be a far worse man than I am, but no matter the situation I shall never be like my elder brother. I'm not ever going to be bitter towards women without reason to be so; my elder brother may assist me in my college courses and help with my studying but he'll never know about you from me or our mother either."

Rachel looks into Noah's eyes as he continues, "Do not worry, Rachel, I am not too open with my elder brother.

His behavior around women isn't pleasant in the slightest which makes him look like a pompous fool whom I don't hold much regard for. I've seen too often what comes of every woman who he gets close to. They become afraid of him and too often come to me for help in escaping his tyranny. It's always for the same reasons too; I am just afraid that one day he'll become abusive toward each and every one of them. Is that too much to be frightened of Rachel?" asked Noah, trying to open up to Rachel and show her that he has better intentions than anyone else she might know.

"In my opinion you've done the right thing Noah," said Rachel, who was beginning to realize that not all men are terribly insufferable, useless, and corrupted to the core, and now she found a truly decent man; You're a good person Noah I can see that in you now."

Rachel, smiling, continues, "You can make an honest lady out of any woman you choose for yourself it's only a matter of time until you find one who you can love without reservations about what should be allowed, and I'm certain that my own father would love for me to choose you as my husband to be."

Chapter Six ~ Chance

Noah continues, "Are you sure Rachel?"

"Yes my father is on a business trip right now but I am willing to let you meet him when he returns, Okay, Noah?"

"Yes I'd like that a lot Rachel, you really are a woman with a lot of depth to your personality, although it is clear that you were a bit preoccupied when we first saw each other. I mean with all those papers in your arms it looked like you were doing some kind of research. Is that about right, Rachel?" asked Noah letting a smile shine through his pondering questions."

"Well yeah I guess you could say that, Noah," Rachel letting down her guard a little to answer him with a straight face.

"I mean with my dreams as they have been lately you'd be doing the same thing as I am now Noah. It's no easy feat trying to get to the bottom of bizarre dreams that haunt me every single night without fail. It's gotten to the point where I have night terrors over them. See where I'm coming from now, Noah?" inquired Rachel with a bit of agitation in her voice, Noah saw the emotion in Rachel's eyes and all the pain those dreams are inflicting upon her.

"It's gotten way too far out of hand for me and if this keeps up, I might end up sick with heavens knows what."

"I see, Rachel, so if you'd like I can give you a check up to make sure nothing more slows you down. Alright, Rachel?"

"Um. Sure, I suppose. Here is my address, Noah. I am available tomorrow after work I usually get out of work around six o'clock in the evening; and I will call you on my way home okay Noah?"

"Sure thing, Rachel. I'd be happy to help you keep your health in perfect condition, promise I'll talk to you tomorrow." Noah said as he wrote down Rachel's cell phone number. A beautiful smile lit up his entire face.

Rachel had taken down Noah's number with the same etiquette that she used for her work and she smiled too with something of an affectionate look on her face.

"Yes call me on your way home. Okay, Rachel? Thanks." Noah said, giving her a knowing smile that would have melted her heart if it already hadn't known what it was that she was thinking.

He was already thinking she was a strong mature woman who could hold her own against anyone else but he knew she wasn't about to give him any grief about whatever needed to be done against all odds. This was it; the time when what mattered most was the health of that woman, even when she seemed to be the healthiest woman around; the outside doesn't always tell the honest truth.

Rachel gave Noah a smile that knew exactly what he was thinking even when he didn't have to say a single solitary word aloud. It was a tricky time for him to think otherwise about the entire matter. It was a whole other ballgame for him to play with a woman like her.

Noah said with a courteous smile, "You're quite a strange lady, but your beauty belies all the magnificent qualities which you hold within your heart."

His blonde hair swung over one broad shoulder and he knew that she was going to be a strong mature woman and it was one thing that appealed to him the most. But there was something more about her; the way she behaved around him that was so alluring that he couldn't help but have special feelings for her.

It was as though he knew her every move before she made it herself which was not something he was used to experiencing around women.

It seemed bizarre at best to describe the dreams as such that would lead to the search for those answers that had eluded her. It seemed as though she was from another time period. Half the time with her timeless beauty and grace, it seemed as if she was a missing piece of his past that couldn't be placed where she was supposed to have been.

Noah knew that there was a reason why he had felt drawn to her from the start, but he didn't know why. Rachel and Noah said their temporary farewells, picked up their coffees, and left the Café. Rachel wanted to believe that it didn't matter if she found out more about her dreams or not, but of course that wasn't the truth. She was more desperate than she'd ever been to find out more about her dreams; her nagging intuition was on the verge of pulling her to Noah and asking him why his eyes are of such a familiar shade of blue.

It was a complicated feeling she pushed out of her mind until she had gotten herself home. Rachel had worked and worked and worked some more until there were answers more than questions. It was something that needed to be figured out.

Rachel knew enough now that she didn't question that the dreams were indeed reality any longer since she found a legitimate name in the papers and books too.

The name that was legitimate was Reigna Valera and the more she let the name linger, the more she said it, the more it made perfect sense that she would ultimately be the reincarnation of Reigna Valera. This seemed to be particularly key to unlocking the reason behind the dreams which have been haunting her sleep every night. It was a name that made sense as the vision of an exquisite beauty with blonde hair and blue eyes. Rachel had given much thought to all the research she had done up to this point. Alas, she had to take a break from all her work and research unless she wanted to overwork herself. This was out of the question for her at this time, but the flash of Noah's blue eyes was the last thing she saw before she lost consciousness.

Noah was working on his homework from college. His older brother, Stephan, had eyes which were like staring directly at an ocean, lit only by sunlight. It was more than that Stephan had realized that his younger brother had fallen in love, which he couldn't accept; to him seeing his younger brother infatuated by a woman. Not at all.

It was their mother who seemed to be the voice of reason, at this point, who really took Noah's side in supporting him; again being surprised at her son for showing interest in a woman older than himself. It was something she never thought she'd ever witness. Noah had paid his older brother no mind after those threats; but alas it had finally happened for her youngest son and really, it seemed that she could be satisfied that Noah found something profound in a woman older than her youngest son.

Meanwhile, Rachel had become more aware of something being very wrong with a feeling of nausea which left her body shaking violently. As intense as it was frightening for her; it was hard for her to sleep after that. It was too much for her to bear.

While trying to fall asleep, Rachel talks to herself:

Now I know that there is something more to my dreams than what I had originally believed, right from the start. It was quite the revelation to be brought to my attention, but alas, it was really quite the intense experience to behold in the most basic sense. I knew that somehow I couldn't outrun the truth fast enough. From that point on, it was really something that had to be considered; but alas, the dreams were intense and knowing that I couldn't stop them was intimidating to say the least. It was something that I wanted nevermore to continue as it was too much, as of now.

Noah could cease all my ailments right now if I just call him. That's what I believed at the time, but right now, this is not the right time. I have work tomorrow and I must be able to go so I can pay my bills. But my health isn't going to take care of itself; if ignored, this could get worse than just nausea. It's too much to withstand at this point, it's not worth losing my job over.

I'm not one to take downtime for an illness. I cannot deal with knowing that my 20-year career with Tiffany's & Company is around the corner. I just want to work normal hours and function well. It's not normal for me to experience nausea of this magnitude and since it comes on so suddenly it doesn't make any sense for me to go through all this nonsense now.

Rachel couldn't bear this suffering any longer it's just too much to deal with. She knew that this illness isn't going to subside all on its own; it has to be dealt with accordingly.

Rachel had reached for her cell phone and called Noah and without warning, she had vomited blood. This was sudden and unexplainable. She sensed that being alone is what is causing the issue most of all.

Noah knew that Rachel couldn't last much longer and he got in his car a Mazda-Five that could've gotten him any girl he wanted, at any given time. Rachel's life was now hanging in the balance of life and death and that was the issue soon to be faced. He could not abandon her to her fate. Rachel was now lying on the bathroom floor with blood flowing steadily from her mouth. The sight devastated Noah when he arrived. He gathered her up into his arms to check her heartbeat and it was faint, her breathing was slow.

Noah swept her into his arms and carried her out to his car and rushed her to the hospital but not before the blood started to flow again from her mouth. He asked for her medical contacts; she tried to tell him to call her father who was on a business trip in Jamaica and Florida, her boss and best friend too.

Noah did all he could to keep her conscious and talking to him which was no trouble at all considering all things that he'd had a hard time with lately. His elder brother, Stephan, wasn't helping keep his temper at an even keel.

Noah got Rachel to the Hospital just before she threw up blood again and he took a tissue from the glove compartment of his car and gave it to Rachel, who was now frail and dangerously close to death's door. He got her to the ER where they had taken her right away when they saw blood dripping from her lip.

Noah knew that she couldn't hold out for much longer and that caused fear to well up in his heart. Noah knew that he could easily lose her the day before a severe disagreement with his elder brother, Stephan, who had forbidden him from chasing love and affection of women. Rachel became the reason and root of the argument between them and now he fears for Rachel's life which is in the balance.

Rachel had given Noah a smile that could break an angel's heart and make many others jealous of her and the affection that she's now receiving from Noah. But it wasn't supposed to be that way and Noah had known this before. Though where he'd known this feeling from, he wasn't so sure as much as he tried to remember where, he just couldn't remember. It was too much for him to work through now and there wasn't any turning back from this event. Rachel had known this and she faced it like she faced every other workday, which pretty much summed up her personality in a nutshell. It certainly didn't seem like something that would involve him, at least until now anyway. Noah was left trying to reevaluate the situation and this time. Rachel wasn't going to face this alone; that was the last thing he'd make her do after this ordeal put her here in the hospital in his care,

Noah knew that it would only be a matter of time until she dies if this doesn't work and seeing Rachel on a stretcher was truly heartbreaking for him to watch. He knew that she might not make it out of here alive and how he'd have to tell her father of her passing which is the most troubling thought he'd ever taken on. This wasn't what he wanted now. He wanted her to live and be fully capable like she was before.

Noah cried silently as Rachel closed her eyes when they took her to the X-Ray Room to find out where the blood is coming from and to see if there's something that can be done about this illness that torments her so much that she spits up blood by the buckets.

She herself knew that if this keeps up that she'd eventually die a slow agonizing death that wasn't supposed to be the end of her life and her career too. It was only a matter of time until the technician came back with the results and she gave Noah a grave once over. It appeared that she had some pretty awful news,

"Noah, Rachel is extremely ill with bleeding from her liver and stomach. I cannot place a cause behind it, though it's a pretty dangerous situation she's in right now."

"Okay so now what?" Noah asked the doctor, choking back tears from the concern he felt for Rachel. The technician told Noah the best way to help her is by staying by her side as she regains control of her body and gets her strength back. The process which will lead to her eventual recovery means that she will need to stay in the hospital for a while until we can get her better.

"Alright then. I'm a medical student taking up my residency so I can graduate from one of the top medical schools in all of NYC," Noah said while being lead into the room where Rachel was now lying unconscious. Seeing her there, had broken Noah's heart into a million pieces.

It wasn't until Rachel opened her eyes that he had smiled willingly, so full of strength that no one could ever imagine." She had wiped away the tears that had fallen down his cheeks in a show of sorrow despite the fact that she had the strength of a saint to endure what she had and know that she might not make it. She was determined to live life to the fullest until the last moment on earth and somehow it was enough to keep her strong only in his presence.

Noah knew she was smiling solely to keep him strong while inside she's suffering so much and having the courage not to show it once, what so ever, even though her aching body was screaming at her, she wasn't going to let it defeat her in this sick game of strength.

Noah had taken it upon himself to stay with her the whole night through and he fell asleep holding her hand tightly all night long, which no one had ever done before.

Somehow it felt good to have someone who had cared that much for her to stay with her as she gets better and healthier. It might seem selfish to her father for someone to put their lives on hold until she returns to her natural vibrant self and now it's Noah to stay with her and even hold her hand through her treatment too. That's more than she would've ever asked for from where she had come, for that would've been just plain cowardice, according to her mother. Her mother died many years ago of something her father wouldn't ever tell her, even though she had asked many times.

Chapter Seven ~ The Knowing

Noah stood up from his seat beside Rachel and gave her a concerned look, then touched her cheek. It was something that gave him a pang of guilt knowing that he still had his mother. It was a sadness that he felt deep in his heart that couldn't be mentioned to anyone considering her health had only worsened since earlier that day. The blood that still dripped from her lip was a deadly reminder to Noah about just why she had been hospitalized in the first place. It didn't make him feel any better about the way he felt about Rachel. She gently pulled at his heartstrings that some of the truth had already come to light. Rachel had gripped tight Noah's hand knowing full well what the attachment would be like if he lost her too soon. Alas, now the best that can be expected of her is to defeat this illness that is eating her alive as if some god-sent miracle was bestowed upon her from birth. This would indeed be extraordinary. Alas, Noah did all he could to be with Rachel as the IV was a steady reminder of the hospital surroundings; a constant reminder of what could be the final night of her life in the making. Seeing Noah tremble as tears filled his eyes, only made her stronger. What choice did she have at this point?

Noah knew that she was becoming responsive to the treatment and she no longer spit up blood. It was time for her to become stronger than the illness and she sensed what seemed to be a lively vibrant light in her heart healing her and she was feeling better; also more alert as well. All this startled Noah, the doctors, and nurses greatly for which no one could find an explanation.

It was as if god was hearing Noah's pleas, not to take her home just yet and that was it. She was feeling more lively than she ever had since her dreams had taken over her waking life. Rachel was fighting for her life and they all knew it. But somehow she was winning against an unknown illness. That alone was proof that god had much bigger plans for her.

Noah was able to bring her home two days later considering her swift recovery but she was ordered not to put any strain on her mind and body. After all no one had an explanation as to why she got better on her own. It was the best she had felt in a while though she wasn't allowed to live alone after that ordeal. So it was best that someone who had known of her ordeal from beginning to end, stay there with her.

Noah had volunteered to allow her to stay at his house while she got back on her feet. While she had gotten into the wheelchair to head out to his car, she told him of the dreams that had triggered such a horrendous illness. Rachel had beamed at Noah as she sat in the wheelchair in front of him, unable to say a single thing to him. Alas, he couldn't help but smile at her in return and somehow at that moment it was all enough, Noah knew that Rachel was quite the independent individual. It was obvious to him now just what was needed for her and her health too. She was happy enough to be out of the hospital. It seemed like weeks since she's been admitted to the hospital. She was happy enough now since she was free to go about her own business even though she was bound to stay at Noah's house until the day that she was able to live again on her own.

Noah caught a glimpse of a cheerful smile on Rachel's face as he signed the discharge papers for Rachel who had grown to almost depend upon him in a way she had never ever depended upon anyone before. Until now, she hadn't ever depended upon anyone even her father as much as she had been as a child. Noah was kind and a very easy man to get along with. Against the will of his elder brother, he was perfectly willing to sacrifice his own life to protect her. It was a feeling of kindness that wasn't ever known to her until now when he had wrapped his arms around her shoulders out of true kindness.

Rachel had smiled serenely as Noah got up and pushed her in her wheelchair out to his car near the hospital entrance. Noah had gotten the car door open in the passenger side and helped her into the car; willingly she took his hand. Noah knew that if his brother Stephan had seen her no doubt he'd treat her most bitterly and he knew that he had to protect her from him. It would have been bad enough if he had to defend her from his demented brother who was so bitter toward women in general, that even their mother was abused by Stephan and he wouldn't have that for Rachel, who was so kind to Noah, though it would so be impossible otherwise.

As soon as they had gotten home, it was a subtle sense of kindness and compassion that had encompassed Rachel and gave her a sense of love and endearment to Noah. It really brought her home to her own senses, to give her a reality of who she had been and who she is now. Noah was not going to allow her to wallow in her own little world much less the research that ended her in the hospital. Rachel was surely one of the best patients Noah had ever seen in his career as a medical student. It would have seemed that Rachel had totally adapted to an entirely different sort of living situation.

Noah knew that he had to keep her severely secret from his brother Stephan. It was imperative that Stephan never find out about Rachel no matter what might happen. Noah knew well enough that Rachel was indeed strong and he had sensed her strength right from the beginning when he saw her at the library, a boundless inner strength even when the odds were stacked against her.

Chapter Eight ~ Inner Strength

Rachel was bold with her feelings and knew that she would still have a home whenever she was ready to return home. It was more efficient for her in a long run; she couldn't believe that she had to stay at a man's house while she's recovering from her illness. It was truly the first time she ever had to be with someone to make sure she didn't have another relapse of her illness. It was enough now for her to believe that he could be one man she could truly trust at the end of the day. Noah was kind and very straight forward with Rachel and somehow it had to unnerve her. She felt it wasn't fair that she couldn't find a way to live with him in his house or in her heart.

Rachel was now in a state of shock when she took notice of just how big his house really was on the inside. She was left truly impressed that he lived there on his own. It really made her feel like she could maybe love him, but again that wasn't something that she couldn't explain on her own. Noah grabbed hold of Rachel's hand and pulled her to himself and knew that he had to keep her safe until she could protect herself. It was enough that her father was out of town on business. It wasn't something that she talked about to outsiders. But this time, she knew that her only other option was to let him into her life and keep in mind that she's only going to be there until she is fully recovered from that awful illness.

Rachel was now feeling a warmth surrounding her heart that was just a firm way of finding out that she and Noah had a past life history. So that would've just made sense. It was something special that held true now it was almost obvious that it was something real which would've been a love real at the end. It was bound to end up like this, against all the odds they had in all the world. Noah was feeling the same thing that Rachel was now feeling; familiar warmth surrounding his heart which was unavoidably strong and comforting too, all at the same time. It was something that couldn't be avoided any longer.

***

Rachel was willing enough to stay with Noah until the day she was strong enough, to once again, live on her own but now she couldn't shake the feeling that someone or something had guided her to this point in her life; something beyond her control or even her understanding. It was enough now to see that Noah was meant to be there for her, for some unseen reason that not even she could understand.

It was time for something else to come about from all of this, time for her inner strength to reawaken, like it had when she was in the hospital. It was now too much to withstand since the light in her heart was so strong. It was miracle enough that she had survived that illness that had overtaken her body. Though she was physically strong for a woman, she still couldn't understand that ailment and how it had come about without warning. It was her inner strength that allowed her to pull through against the odds that were clearly against her.

***

Rachel was just starting to come to see clearly the home that had been arranged for her recovery time and smiled idly to herself as she thought *my goodness I had worried about settling down with a man before all this. Now I haven't a choice but to consider this home until I'm fully recovered from that awful ailment that had me laid up in that god-awful hospital bed.* Noah hadn't left Rachel's side once. It was an intense time for them both but again it was also the first time anyone other than her mom had stayed with her.

Noah was kind to Rachel all the while as he had gotten her settled into his house for the first day but she was unnervingly happy, which didn't seem like her at all. Was it all a ruse to hide some sort of secret he knew for this to happen - if the patient is in enough pain? But somehow it seemed a little too perfect; a smile that graced her lips as pink as rose buds.

It didn't bother him at all with that sort of business. He'll figure her out while she's under his roof. It was all a matter of time until the truth came out. Rachel was genuinely satisfied with sitting on his plush sofa sipping hot tea. It was something she had taken comfort in somewhere along the way. It didn't seem like her at all. On a normal basis, it would've been a piping hot cup of coffee that seemed to be the obvious choice for a woman of her position. It would've been enough with that story to earn her a scolding from Noah.

Rachel had finished her cup of tea and decided to get some well-deserved sleep, even though her better nature decided against it and wanted her to do at least a check on her email for work. But against her better nature, she went to her bedroom and settled down for some well-deserved sleep that her body so desperately needed. It was hours until she woke up for supper. She had gone down stairs to see Noah making supper for them both. Rachel knew that he was a rather talented man. It didn't occur to her that she was living with him until then still it suited her taste for men. At least she didn't expect to see him working so hard around the house for her comfort. Nonetheless she couldn't just sit back and let a man do all the preparations for supper; she had to let herself into the kitchen, which was larger than she had first expected. But she knew her way around any kitchen. She saw that he was making a Greek salad which was in her mind, her expertise indeed. It was a better planned meal than she originally gave him credit for.

Noah was pretty sure that Rachel hadn't cooked or even made a salad a day in her life, apparently he was mistaken. She had a hand at chopping the lettuce and slicing the olives and the tomatoes. That was the easy part in her opinion. Rachel didn't just do the slicing, and she prepared the Greek dressing as well. Noah was planning a bit of a surprise for the main course, Rachel's favorite dish, rack of lamb with mint jelly was on the menu and that would shock her for sure. Rachel was working hard on the Greek salad and Noah was checking the lamb often. Noah knew that Rachel was used to hard work since she was used to living alone but he knew that she was quite experienced in the kitchen regardless, of where it was. In the long run, it was lucky that she was able.

Rachel knew that she had just woken up from her rest. It just didn't make any sense that she was here to recover but she knew that it would've earned her a scorning from her doctors for her wanting to get something done for herself. It was all the same to her if she knew her body as well as others said she had.

She thought the lamb was in the oven and the Greek salad dressing was done; she did her part in the kitchen. Now she needed to take it easy until supper was ready. It was a wonder she had lasted for as long as she had. It was more than she needed to get herself better.

It was more than a matter of time until she had gotten some series of flashbacks, of something that was almost too bizarre to be truly understood ... by anyone else on earth. Noah also had gotten some flashbacks while making supper. It was almost as if Rachel and he had connected mentally about living and thriving in a civilization that had been lost to time. Now he knew that he might be going crazy with these visions. Rachel gave him a concerned look as though she knew what had just run through his mind because she saw the same lost civilization that was still so beautiful and thriving with temples that were in pristine condition, indeed.

Chapter Nine ~ Secrets

Noah hadn't wanted Rachel to be concerned about him since they had seen the same thing at the same time. It was enough for them both; while they were cooking they had somehow connected to each other. Rachel was just as willing as Noah to try to recover from her ailment. It gave them time to get to know each other. In the meantime the lamb was being cooked and it wasn't long afterwards that the lamb finished cooking and Noah placed the lamb on the plates in generous proportions with the mint jelly atop the lamb. They had finished supper now truly satisfied with that decent meal. Noah did something to put Rachel's comforts ahead of his own and brought Rachel her tea on the sofa where she sat and she sipped her tea patiently.

Noah knew that Rachel was kind and now rather frail, yet she was slowly regaining her strength. Her stamina was more than enough now. It didn't make any sense, he had thought to himself. It was all more than he could bear at any rate. It now was just a matter of time until something within him made him think it was something other than a scientific illness, although he had a separate belief that some things just cannot be explained away. It was a long day for them both and they both had known it too. As always, Rachel was a lovely woman whose sense of timing was more than he could ever ask for in a woman.

Rachel knew that she wouldn't be able to hide the truth from Jessica or Rose much longer. It was time that she stopped denying what was going on in her life. It was nearly inevitable that something be said to both of them. In due time it can no longer be kept secret since she had worked hard to maintain her reputation of being unapproachable by men. It was not her place to jeopardize that part of herself. It was of utmost importance that she be able to keep that part to herself; nonetheless Rachel never gave into the expectations that had caved in around her heart and spirit. Somehow it was all enough for them both.

Noah had allowed Rachel to finish her after-dinner tea then swept her up into his arms and carried her back to bed where she fell fast asleep the moment he laid her down. Noah took some deep breaths before leaving her to rest peacefully in the guest bedroom he had given to her while she stayed with him during her recovery. It was a simple gesture full of the ultimate kindness one could ever express in anyway acceptable.

Noah was a man with a strong enough heart to act upon that kindness. It was more than enough at that point to make him realize what it was that he had felt for her all along. He had grown to love her in such a short amount of time, but he had loved her and he knew what it was that he had to do after she recovered from her illness.

Rachel was the most beautiful creature that he had ever laid eyes upon in his nineteen years of life. It was more than a gift to have ever met her in the first place; it was his good karma in doing so much good for others that brought her into his life. Noah was moved to tears when he realized that she had been someone special to him right from the beginning and she was willing to accept him back into her life … without another favor to be asked of him in return.

Chapter Ten ~ Double Life

Noah knew that it was Rachel that he was meant to be with after all that wasted time. It was something that he never thought he'd have time for, yet here she is and he knew that it wasn't a dream,

Rachel really is here in his house. It was an opportunity he was never allowed because of Stephan, the reason most ladies he brought home had been frightened off and now … here's a new one who could be equally intimidating by his brother. "Well now this is a good thing indeed; Rachel was more than just a pretty face and that's something else to be rather proud of in a special sense," thought Stephan to himself, as he closed the door behind him.

He went off to his own room like he often did after he stopped in his office to finish up some homework at the last minute. Then he powered down his laptop and went to his bedroom and went right to sleep. While he was fast asleep he suddenly realized why he had indeed fallen in love with her. It was because the one dream he had just experienced was covered with images of a lovely lady who looked remarkably like Rachel, but no where was a Temple that was snow white marble with bronze and golden statues that had nearly stunned him out of his sleep. Rachel had been asleep in the guest room which was just one more thing that kept him calm and from screaming from the shock of seeing blood in that same dream as well.

The next day Rachel had awakened as refreshed as she would have normally. She got up and made breakfast for Noah since he had overslept. She had gone to his room to wake him up and said that he had slept over an hour later than usual. She knew that she had usually awakened rather early for work; but now, it seems that since she had been temporarily put on recovery leave Noah got up rather early, ready for the day doing his part to keep his calm not to discourage Rachel from doing anything kind for him. As a kind gesture just the same, Noah was more than willing to have breakfast with Rachel after all he had done to make her comfortable in his home.

"It was only a matter of time until he realized she was the woman from his dream the night before and what was so wrong with that," he wondered. But the fact was that it would eventually interfere with his studies and his work. Stephan was a big enough obstacle, threatening to stand in his way of loving her the way she deserved to be loved. It was more than enough for them both. But alas it was a sign of something beautiful yet to come. Either way, it was more than Noah could've ever asked for, without a doubt in his mind. It was truly a dream come true for him to endure witnessing; but Rachel had known enough of his thoughts to know what he was indeed thinking, without him saying a single word.

Chapter Eleven ~ The Evidence

Rachel stared at Noah with wide eyes and an open mouth and Noah knew that she had heard his thoughts loud and clear. Yet somehow, it was more acceptable since she had known. Rachel was slowly becoming a more reasonable lady. Somehow he seemed to be so lonely as he had been before she walked into his life. Rachel had offered Noah a clearer view of what was truly meant to be inspite of his elder brother's protesting. It was fate that they were destined to be together as a couple who remained stronger together against the storms of life; something that Noah didn't expect from her in the least, but here she was offering this up to him.

Noah knew that Rachel was someone special after just a brief moment of gazing into her clear blue eyes. It was something amazing beyond any explanations, acceptable to him but clearly this was beyond comprehension. Rachel wasn't a naïve little girl, since she was six feet four inches tall, she was in no way a small child any longer all legs and a slender form to show off the woman she had become. Noah knew that Rachel was truthfully a free spirit beyond the shadow of a doubt he knew that she was definitely strong and truly independently free from the expectations that others desired of her.

Rachel wasn't one to speak out about her dreams or what she looked for in a man and this was enough for her to bottle up her feelings. Somehow, she was starting to see something radiant in Noah's midnight blue eyes that shined with a sense of calm that she had only felt while sitting by the harbor watching the boats and ships come in and going out. This was the calmest she'd ever felt since then; rare indeed but Rachel knew that Noah was always going to be near her watching over her making sure that she was okay.

Rachel knew that Noah was having the same dream as she was. Somehow, she was able to read him like a book. It wasn't right ... not even remotely close. She was getting the feeling that she was making this into a seriously wrong type of text book, but alas, she was able to see the truth in his midnight blue eyes and that was enough of that from her thoughts. She had instantly put those thoughts out of her mind. Noah was trying to hide the thoughts going through his mind too but still he couldn't hide anything from Rachel; her charm had him at her mercy and somehow, that only made their relationship more indescribable to him or to anyone for that matter. It didn't seem right to him at all.

Later that day Noah went off to Med School and allowed Rachel to stay at home and rest. It was the kindest act she'd ever experienced in most of her own life; it was something that she never thought he'd allow her to do no matter how much time had passed between them, this was the best that had ever come about. Rachel had been kind to Noah all the while and yet it was more than he alone could ever ask for - still it was perfect just the way it worked out.

Chapter Twelve ~ Truth

The Professors at the Medical School knew that Noah had a houseguest he was taking care of. This made it a little easier in a long run; still it was necessary to go to class. Rachel remained in the back of his mind the whole time while he was in Anatomy class and studying Cardiology which was one of the more complex subjects he had taken. Still he had his homework that night to complete.

When Noah had gotten home later that night with some of her belongings, such as her laptop and some extra clothes, she was rather pleased that he was that thoughtful of her. This was the best to be expected, to say the least of him. It was more than she really wanted anyway.

Rachel had thought well of Noah; he had gone to get her laptop and its adapter also her cell phone. She knew that knowing him was a gift. The only other person who had done such acts of kindness was her mother, in times past. She knew that there were secrets hidden from her since childhood. Rachel had known that her mother had abandoned them for a reason but it wasn't ever brought up as it was taboo to even speak of. The secrets being kept from her caused an eerie feeling to creep up into her heart that had made her think about the many reasons she had to have that feeling creeping into her heart.

The dreams she's been having have had the keys to the many secrets that have surrounded her entire life, from beginning to present day. It was enough to make her wonder if the keys were that plain to see in her dreams, even now. It wasn't ever supposed to be mentioned as it was a taboo to even bring up in her family. So asking her father about it was out of the question and that was that. So she just closed her eyes, took a deep breath and exhaled, opened her eyes and everything seemed so much clearer than before; when she felt like she was walking in a daze but it all cleared up so swiftly that it didn't even matter in the end.

Noah was staring at Rachel and thought she was so deep in thought he knew she was indeed alright. Even he knew well enough to leave a lady alone when she's like that or he might be sorry. It seemed that Rachel was indeed deep in thought due to the fact that she didn't have a clue that Noah was staring at her rather hard. It was what it was and Noah being the kind one that he was, just let her be. Finally Rachel came back to her senses about three hours later just before supper was ready. Noah had prepared her dinner for her when she was deep in thought; she smiled at him knowing that there will be many more challenges ahead in their lives. It wasn't going to be an easy road for them either. Somehow it didn't bother either one of them.

Noah didn't want this to end, this beautiful relationship that was practically around the corner from where they're at now in their lives. It seemed right at the time for Noah to take Rachel in his arms, as strong as he was, and held her close to him and she couldn't push him away. The warmth was indeed familiar to her. It was as if she had already felt this feeling before. It was enough to bring tears to her eyes; this was what Rachel had long since longed for. It was a precious moment between the two of them, the warm embrace she had found herself in was more than what she was used to, but she gave into his warmth.

Chapter Thirteen ~ Honesty Revealed

Rachel never imagined that she'd ever find herself in the arms of a man. It was something that she solely avoided. It was a special time for her now, to find herself enjoying the warmth that had surrounded her. Noah felt his own heart race as he felt Rachel melt in his arms, and knowing that she had never had this before, made him feel twice as lucky. Indeed, it was a moment between the two of them that would never be forgotten by him or by Rachel herself.

She knew that Noah meant well by keeping her in his arms, strong and warm, but it was something that Rachel had well avoided, until now. She gave herself enough time in his arms to get used to the feeling and the scent of him, so familiar, that she could've sworn that she'd caught this scent before, in the past, but she knew better than that.

Noah knew that Rachel was not used to such fair treatment of her kind heart but still it seemed all too much for her to endure. In due time, it seemed like Rachel was starting to adapt to having a man embrace her. Still she wanted to feel something real. It was all enough as of now. She felt the kindness in her heart well up and tears escaped her eyes, her beautiful blue eyes which were expressing the kindness deep within her own good heart. It was now good enough for her to shed tears over; it was a fair way to act at this time.

Rachel saw now that she couldn't ever return to the life she had once known as it was a meager way to live life. It couldn't leave much else to be desired because she'd often frightened most every other man off with death glares. It was Noah who had melted her icy heart when he first embraced her. Noah knew that she wouldn't cave into just anyone who had become someone so dear. Heaven knows just how deep it really ran with Rachel. She could never really fall in love. It seemed enough for her. Noah was determined to make sure she stayed true to herself and her own beliefs.

Now it was solely time for her to check up on her emails which had been sitting on her computer for days and weeks. Now she really needed to get things done and be a little more productive. Noah knew that she'd have to do this eventually and she did it without fail. Rachel was rather diligent in her work. Noah knew that she was just as hard a worker as he himself. He hadn't ever made any serious errors in judgment when it mattered most. She had loved her work longer before they'd even met. It was indeed something that had paid her well for all her services. But somehow it made her life something extremely special. This was indeed a special time in their lives. This whole ordeal was cementing their relationship into something solid and made every day worth getting up for.

Noah was gifted in terms of intuition and considering all things else, it was a fate predetermined according to a recent dream that she too had in the past couple nights. Noah was more determined than ever to see where this relationship will go in the future. It was something worthwhile looking into for their sake but somehow made everyday more pleasant for the workaholic Rachel, who nearly never took a break from work. It was a busy life style for them both. She knew her limits, whether she was working too hard or just pacing herself in working her own way. Somehow it was enough to just get her through the day.

***

Noah was a true gentleman. He knew when to give Rachel her space so that she could work twice as hard as what he's personally used to himself. It was indeed a gift that he had found such a fine lady as Rachel to love and forever be faithful, even when Stephan, his elder brother, threatened to stand in the way. It's enough to make them all the stronger together. It really had made the difference in Rachel's life, meeting Noah and now staying with him until her illness entirely subsides, and she can look after herself like she had before.

But again, would she really want to when she can have Noah looking after her day in and day out? Of course she'd miss living out on her own. Then again, what would be good for her well-being?

Rachel had always been a rather intelligent woman, but still, a kind woman with a lot of generosity in her heart. It was something that was meant to be; something truly special. Indeed it had always been a precious thing that lived deep in Rachel's heart. Noah knew that it was a feeling that was beyond the shadow of a doubt, grow ever deeper and ever more solid; with just the right amount of love and the proper amount of kindness that would undoubtedly deepen as time passes between them.

Noah was thankful for her graciousness (make no mistake about that at all). Still it only made that much sense to them both as he sat quietly watching her calm focused actions on her laptop. She worked as hard as he ever had in his studies. It only caused her to care more and somehow, that alone was enough, as it ever was, for them to be forever happy together. It was without another word that Rachel glanced up at him lovingly and smiled with much passion in her eyes. Noah could not resist knowing her more and seeing that her work was long and hard, returning many emails from her clientele and her boss; also her best friend took much of her time to respond, so it made some sense to him that she do so much at once. All it really took was some mild understanding on his part to allow them to make it this far into their soon to be happy future together.

It seemed that hope for the future had blossomed in Rachel's heart as she spotted Noah watching her work, ever diligently over her laptop, to get some of the emails sent back. Many were concerned, her friends at work and even her boss. It was something she'd expected at this point, but again never this many emails all at once. It seemed the best she could do was to reply to several emails. Over the past few hours as she continued to answer many emails from the clientele, rather lengthy to read and reply to, Rachel did it with the usual poise and grace that she had shown at work. She continued to be courteous to all the clientele. Her boss had stressed her to be with all clientele when she first started her job at Tiffany's & Company, Noah knew that Rachel was quite the hard worker in her own right, but alas, it was Rachel who had considered Noah to be the hard worker in the long run.

Chapter Fourteen ~ Limits

Rachel was a hard worker with a penchant for the arts, but alas, she was strong and a hard worker for Tiffany's & Co. She had never felt so strongly about anyone the way she felt for Noah. Noah was not the type of man to abandon hope for a lady like Rachel, who was more than hopeful to eventually have him in her life until the end she was extremely kind and very, very fair indeed with all her work.

She never took anything for granted in her life due to the fact that any day could very well be her last day. She knows that love is rather a rare thing for her to find. She did find something real that was not to be mistaken for lust but she had given every care to the last of it all. It was something special to them both it was enough now.

Noah was a diligent man who had worked tirelessly to graduate from medical school. It was a better living than he could possibly want over time; it was seriously becoming a part of his daily life. Rachel was a skilled woman who had given most care to those around her, even when the odds seemed to be stacked against them. She knew better than to allow anyone to interfere with her plans for the future and somehow that was fine she thought to herself, as she replied to countless emails. It was a gift she never thought she was worthy of and that was that.

Rachel took swift glances up at Noah through long dark eyelashes that were long enough and attractive enough to make anyone think that she was wearing false ones. It was "au natural" in the French term. She returned his feelings too. She was willing to give him half a chance to set their feelings straight; it was a more willing way to live at this point. Still she had cared for Noah and somehow it was already Rachel who was strongest when she was looking to Noah for love.

Rachel was seriously working towards a peaceful life with Noah and now she knew that a piece of her was longing for another way to live with the only man she had ever had a connection, in such a short amount of time. It was enough for her to love him silently until her dreams had returned a couple of nights later. It was still an alarming one to experience time and again, even when Noah was near; she knew that it was going to be the rest of her entire life these dreams are trying to awaken the truth that was concealed from her. But alas, it wasn't to be kept from her for her entire life. Rachel knew better than to allow her dreams to take over her entire body. Whether she wanted it or not, it was bound to happen somehow. It was going to happen and that was her fate to be realized in due time.

Chapter Fifteen ~ Flight of Truth

Noah was taking notice of Rachel's odd behavior over breakfast the next day, of course some things had been kept from him, also since early childhood. But naturally he had forgotten about some of those peculiar things that once had been said to him by his mother. Even then he had sometimes acted as if he were from a different time period and it occasionally frightened his mother and angered his elder brother Stephan. His father was usually shocked by the behavior quirks that he had possessed since he was young.

Rachel seemed to have similar quirks like he used to possess but alas her father had over looked her quirkiness which was what secretly frightened her mother and hence the reason why she had left her with her father.

Rachel was still in possession of her quirk of being rather noble and still never able to allow others to suffer in times of need. It was a gift of empathy and still she was sensitive to other worldly spirits which no one else could see or sense. This was where her gift had brought her, but even though that might have been the case, she wasn't one to leave the future alone without real answers to the questions that had haunted her every waking hour. It was real and she had known this. It was more than enough to keep the truth intact of what was possible, even in times of harsh treatment of others and Noah knew that her quirk was indeed unique in its own way.

Noah realized it was all real and now his quirk had resurfaced and he became rather curt. He knew that the truth was about to come to light before his eyes; it was a divine gift from the heavens above that this was what his mother tried to conceal from him since he grew up into a man of true intelligence and skill. It was real; the truth had been released from Rachel the woman sitting before him in the kitchen having her morning coffee. Noah poured his coffee and sat down with her and they talked about the quirks they were gifted with over time. It was a precious time they had that day and truths well-hidden had been brought to light.

All secrets reveal themselves over time, but this time, it was Rachel who realized all the things were hidden from them for a reason and it was something that shouldn't have taken place. Noah was now worried that this could affect the life he had always desired for himself, but because of Rachel, he knew where it was that he belonged. He belonged in her arms as warm and forgiving as any god or goddess that had ever been mentioned in all history books. It was true that he had loved Rachel. Now he had to live up to that love, which was strong enough to disrupt time and space.

It was their love that had been realized over time. Now it was time that Rachel tell him all she had known, all along, since those dreams had returned to finish what needed to be done right. It was the honesty that had been the truth all along. It was time that secrets are revealed and time heals the deep wounds that had been of the past, nothing more or less.

It was time that Rachel set herself free from her reservations about falling in love with the right man. No one else could be the one she could be herself around and now it was time that Noah sees the same as she can. No one else could understand the quirks that make them different according to society and that made them true individuals that could make the difference in the modern world and set them free from what binds them to the world they had known.

Noah was no longer apprehensive about being near Rachel the woman who could set him free from all the chains that had kept him hostage in the modern world but it was what he knew and loved in Rachel that had become something precious in him let come whatever may. It was love, an unquenchable affectionate love, that no one could ever come between them, even if heaven and earth threatened to tear them apart. It was indeed a love blessed by the universe itself.

Rachel had then revealed to Noah that they are star children and Noah knew the term of star children from dreams and the children born of stars had another name and

Rachel knew this as well as he had THEY WERE CALLED ATLANTEANS - that was their true given name.

It was more than even Noah could ever imagine. As of now, it was truly time for a genuine awakening from their long since dead identities, that were lost so long ago at the bottom of the Atlantic ocean. It was something that Noah couldn't possibly make up on his own, but Rachel at his side really gave him real insight about why their quirks make them so different. It's more than what any of them could see was true. It was based primarily on the research that Rachel had started. But as the dreams had progressed, it revealed more than either of them had deemed appropriate in that short time. It was Noah who had been quirky since birth, but alas, so was Rachel who was older than he was by a mere seven years. Still she had given him the truth behind who they truly were in a previous life, though where they had once lived, no longer existed on the map.

Rachel was no longer one to be too serious in his presence but she smiled willingly and she acted more naturally than she ever had in her life. It was as if the real her was being released from within her, out into the world around her. Her eyesight had sharpened to the point where all the colors around her were more vivid than they'd ever been, even when she didn't wear contact lenses or glasses. Her eyes were now seeing every detail in full color as if her eyes had dulled over time, but now, it was as if the Atlantean within her had given her the appropriate eyesight of the woman within herself. It was truly a miracle that they were both still capable human beings in spite all their hardships.

Chapter Sixteen ~ Atlantis Revealed

Noah finally understood where it was that he had lived long ago. They now understood that Rachel was always meant to be his, right from the start; it was she who had seen the truth come to light with the brilliance of starlight that shines vividly on cloudless nights.

It was best now that he himself had come to know the truth of why he was reincarnated into a modern-day man who had loved his Rachel more than words could ever say. That is why everything turned out as well as the gods and goddesses had planned but again. They were Catholics now and they were never again to worship other gods.

Rachel was willing to accept the truth revealed unto her through her dreams. It only made sense that way, Rachel had never known a more brilliant truth than the one she had just recently come to know. It was no longer the secret that would destroy her but become the truth that would make her stronger and keep her whole for the remainder of her life. It was truth that set her and Noah free, make no mistake on that, because she was a fighter and Noah knew how to heal her and keep her safe, though she herself had the knowledge of a sage and somehow magic in her blood still lived on, as part of her quirk, it was just as well that be.

Noah wasn't weak anymore with Rachel being at his side during this time of hardship and still it made sense for him to love her, more than ever, before it really had made the sense that he began to understand why his parents fought for him to have a normal life. It was enough for Rachel too, just to live with Noah and remain strong when he's this close that she could feel his affection for her from across the kitchen table. It was best this way, no doubt about that anymore. Noah knew that Rachel was the one to make everything alright again in both their lives. Make no mistakes about that anymore; it was the master plan to live a healthy happy life with her at his side.

Rachel was the strongest woman that Noah had ever known in all his life. She was more than he had ever hoped for in his life. It was a precious time in his life when love was only when he was with Rachel; it was she who had felt this just as strongly as they both had now.

It was up to them where this relationship leads in time; never had she ever felt a kindness in a man as genuine as Noah, the man who is now officially a part of her life and nothing less. It was a genuine feeling of kindness and real affection that no one could ever understand, even if they had tried to do so.

This time Noah knew that Rachel was the real deal and he was determined to have Rachel in his life even, when his wretched older brother was bound and determined, to drive away every female that got close to Noah. It was now joyous to have Rachel in his life proud and healthy too.

It was the only thing he had ever longed for, the gift of love that drove him in his studies at school and she was still rather kind to him even when she didn't yet have the strength to go to work at Tiffany's & Co. leaving the comfort of the house that Noah had let her live with him in. All the while, it was too perfect for him to have met a woman as divine as Rachel. It was as if someone out there had wanted Rachel and Noah to meet right from the start. It was a week until she had regained her full strength and was able to attend work like she would normally do on her daily basis.

The light that shown around her heart as she worked was a brilliant light; even Noah had taken true notice of her heart had a vivid and pale pink light around it the whole time. She had missed her friend Jessica and her boss Rose for whom she had worked so diligently even in all the tough times she had endured. It was the best that had been offered even when it all mattered so little. It was time she attended to work after such a long absence, but now, it was time that Rachel releases the times within herself. Noah knew enough of her now that it was all true it was time to see the truth.

Rachel had prepared herself for the next day going back to work for Tiffany's. It was something that really was quite important. It was time that she became a devoted worker and girlfriend but still she knew the truth. It was the best outcome that could become her in the end of all that could be real; in both their lives. It's right that she feels as she does about the work that she loves most in life.

It matters more now than it ever had, out of all the times that had come and gone, it sets all things straight. Rachel got up early the next day, got ready for work, had her coffee and she was capable of heading out to work in high heels. It was finally time that she regained her independence; she went to work with her purse and laptop and had arrived at work early before everyone else. She had gotten to her office and opened her laptop; and replied to many of her clients emails and she hadn't ever wavered in answering every last one. It seemed that she had done her part in working ultimately hard. She hadn't ever wavered as she had worked as hard as she did to keep up her work.

Chapter Seventeen ~ Stephan

Not a half an hour after Rachel started work Rose, her boss, had walked in taking notice of all the work she had done thus far. She was quite impressed with Rachel and all the energy she had, which left Rose concerned soon enough. Jessica had walked in and saw Rachel's work getting done at maximum speed. It was as if she had suddenly gotten a massive amount of energy and she knew it was what happens with caffeine, but this time was different.

She was different; no doubt about that anymore. It was almost as if love had become her sole energy source after such a long long time. Rachel looked up at Jessica and let out a slight laugh, which was far from the Rachel she had known beforehand. It was clear now that something had happened in her absence that transpired this change.

While the day went on as usual, something unusual had happened; a tall blonde-haired man with deep blue eyes stalked over to Rachel's desk. Rachel looked up and asked what his name was. He gave an intimidating smile and said, "My name is Stephan Levier, the elder brother of Noah and you'll not see my brother again or I shall personally kill you for even associating with him."

Now this had Rachel fuming saying, "If you're Stephan then Noah had already warned me about you and your violent tendencies. It seems your brother was right on about that."

Jessica was just hoping and praying he was a good guy which obviously wasn't the case. It seemed that Stephan was as violent tempered as Noah had said he was, exactly. Rachel sent a telepathic message to Jessica warning her to stay away or he'd kill her too. That really frightened Jessica to no end. It was the one time Rachel had ever wished that she'd stayed in bed but now it seemed that Rose was trying to stand up for her like the loyal friend she is.

Despite all the trouble that Stephan had brought to Rachel that day, Jessica was starting to worry much more than usual about her own life. Rachel was just starting to restore hers to its former glory. It was a worse time than ever for her to know that Noah was in class but here stood Stephan, that wretched elder brother that had thus far made Noah miserable. It was an unfair treatment that couldn't ever be taken back.

Jessica was not one to fight but she was without a doubt protective of her very best friend who had been victimized by circumstances that were not at all her own fault. It wasn't fair that Rachel be treated this way but without a doubt she was not going to just stand by and leave this to her very best friend, which was clearly enough now that she had realized just the sort of danger that Rachel was in.

It wasn't going to just go away overnight this time. It was a lasting mark that was to be a blemish upon a pure soul that had belonged to Rachel, her very best friend. It was now to be a mark that would drive Stephan to wanting to kill Rachel himself. It was best that this be kept a secret from all, the honesty that remains best, after all this nonsense has taken place at work.

Rose was one defensive boss and she was now sure that Rachel was in some very big trouble with Stephan. It was not something she was familiar with, but again she was very aggressive against those who threaten her friends and employees. It wasn't fair that Rachel suffer this terrible behavior and she knew that she may have to let go of her finest sales executive; due to the threat that is Stephan. It was a fearful feeling that she hadn't ever known before in her entire life. It wasn't right for this to happen. It was not something that she ever wanted to experience ever again. This was the last act of kindness that Rachel would ever receive from Rose.

Jessica knew that Rachel would be leaving Tiffany's & Co. due to what had just taken place in Rachel's own office. It was clearly a nightmare that she had prayed was just a nightmare and nothing more. It was one thing to endure this hardship. It was another to actually endure it firsthand. Jessica was already in tears when she had come to know that

Rachel was leaving them all. It wasn't something that she had wanted for her very best friend to experience this time.

It was because of that brute Stephan who had cursed and threatened her. It wasn't enough that he had caused her very best friend to lose her job but it nearly left Rachel a broken woman; which was indeed what was happening at this point. It was the worst shape Jessica had ever seen Rachel in. It was enough to make her want to comfort Rachel in her time of need it was a painful thing to see this time.

Rose knew all too well how Rachel was feeling at this point. It was as if the stars had suddenly turned against her in her time of need. This hardship had come to be the worst time of Rachel's entire life. It was such a terrible thing for Rose to see in her eyes but the secret was clear and it was another thing for her to see right in front of her now; for both Jessica and Rose to help Rachel find a new job.

It was too much for even her to withstand; it was a time of great distress for Rachel that day.

It wasn't what she had wanted of her day, it was just plain painful, not knowing what to expect of her daily life anymore. It was more of an untimely circumstance than she would have personally liked, to say the absolute of things as they were now. It was not what she would've imagined as of now. It was a true nightmare realized; Jessica was the one to calm Rachel down when hardship strikes hardest in her best friend's life. It was not for the faint of heart to contend with after all. The worst is over, there is nothing left but the aftermath of the worst of it.

Jessica wasn't one to abandon her friends who were indeed at a loss so great it could shake the very foundation of Rachel's life and even when the world seemed to be coming to an end. Jessica was always there to keep the best memories alive and reminded her to never lose hope in the future as it has not been written yet in terms of knowing what the future held at this point.

It was Rachel who grew stronger with every single hardship that crossed her way. Rose kept Rachel and Jessica calm and together found a way to allow her to keep her job and still evade trouble that was Stephan. It was a worthwhile attempt to keep everything together at least until she can find another occupation that she could do in her original form not being distinguished from the career she had once before.

But Rachel had come to see that this might be the only hope she has left of having her beloved career another day but still it seemed as if she had just slipped through a very close call.

It was as if all time had ceased to be a part of the ultimate truth. It was truly enough for her to hold out over such an amount of time but alas it was part of the truth that she had always done the right thing. It was more than enough to live with even if all else went wrong it was just a part of the chance that Rachel had at this point of time.

Chapter Eighteen ~ Rachel

Rachel had done her part in keeping calm even while the force of Stephan's threat had still hung in the air, thicker than anything anyone could ever imagine. It was the worst she could want. Rachel was bound and determined to set everything right against one man who could ruin the love that Noah and she had shared. It seemed to only become stronger against the darkness that followed her around ever since Stephan threatened her at work. It was now just a matter of time until something huge happens, even if it takes a lifetime.

Later that day after work, when Noah had come to pick her up, she let out a tremendous sigh of relief since it was a threat made against her life by that dolt of an elder brother Stephan. It was not nearly enough to say it was just that she was glad that work was over for the day.

Rachel knew that Noah did not realize that she had a rather tough day at work. He could not understand why, at least not yet anyway. He was rather calming to Rachel and her nerves, which could sooth away even the most frazzled. It seemed that he was quite talented in keeping her strong and capable of holding her own against all, that had stood against them both. It was rather intense now than it ever was.

It's best that what matters most of all, she knows whatever may happen, will happen.

If Noah knows best of what had come to pass it seems as if Rachel had given Noah only subtle hints about what was about to happen to her, if they weren't so careful. Alas it was time that she lay her head down upon Noah's shoulder for comfort.

It was truly enough indeed as Noah had been quite independent all his life. When hardship was clearly upon them both they were just as loving as they'd always been in the past.

Acknowledgements

I am extremely grateful and thankful to all my friends and family who have encouraged me to do my best.

I wish to thank the members of the Lewiston Writers' Group for their ongoing support and suggestions throughout my book-writing project.

About the Author

Rachel is an avid reader of romance novels and mythology. She drew upon these genres to create *The Determination of the Atlantean Race*.

Rachel Brown, Author.

Made in the USA
Monee, IL
20 January 2020